Introduction

This tutor can be used for teaching position skills or for practising those already learned. Before beginning, students need to be able to read and play—in tune—in many different keys in first position, and to confidently use their 4th finger.

Finger numbers are kept to a minimum. Tunes played in a single position have fingering at the beginning of each staff as a useful reminder. Pieces with shifts generally have only the shifts fingered. More fingering may be pencilled in as needed.

Simple bowings are used and tempi and expression marks have been omitted to focus on developing skill and confidence in position playing.

Moving around the fingerboard

From the earliest lessons, explore the fingerboard! Try left hand pizzicato with different fingers in different positions. Play glissando games along a string on all fingers or any one: sirens, ghostly music, bird songs, donkey brays, train whistles; at reduced pressure or harmonic level, perhaps incorporating these sounds into appropriate tunes.

Glissando on each finger up to the octave harmonic on each string and back again. Experiment with changing between an open string, its octave harmonic, and its octave on the upper string.

Play games using these sounds: 'copycat', 'be my echo', 'violin conversations', playing by ear. These activities will help develop a relaxed, free, flexible left arm and hand and pave the way for position work.

Playing in different positions by rote and by ear

Once a major scale and arpeggio starting on 1st finger and using 4th finger have been learnt, sing and play by ear tunes in 1st position then again in other positions.

These three note tunes can use fingers 1, 2, 3 or 2, 3, 4:
Hot cross buns; *Burnt buns* (minor *Hot cross buns*); *Merrily we roll along*; *Suogan*; *Cobbler, cobbler mend my shoe* and the other *soh, mi* chants.

The four note tunes are *Pease pudding hot*; *Boil 'em cabbage down*; *Rain, rain go away* and other *soh, mi, lah* tunes. Otherwise, play suitable fragments such as the beginning of *Row, row, row your boat* or *Au clair de la lune*. Play a 1st finger one octave scale and arpeggio in different positions. Then try longer, easy well-known tunes: *Mary had a little lamb*; *Twinkle, twinkle little star*; *Frère Jacques*.

Music can be repeated at the same pitch in fifth position on a lower string, or transposed an octave. Play a three or four note tune or fragment starting on low 1st finger, then shift up a tone (whole step) or semitone (half step) and play again. Repeat up and down a string, playing in different keys. If wished, the names of the notes used may be named.

Play in first position by rote and by ear, using finger numbers before note names, ahead of learning to read in the new position. Play target practice games: swap between 3rd finger in first position and 1st finger in third position on E, A or D strings and check intonation against the open string below. Match the 2nd finger in third position on the G, D and A strings to the open string above. Listen for how a note in tune causes the corresponding open string to ring in sympathy.

Include easy shifts in well-known tunes that could be played on one string instead of crossing strings. Sing the interval before shifting. Start with shifting during rests or while playing an open string. The 'e-i-ee-i-oh' of *Old MacDonald had a farm* can be played in 3rd position. Try same finger shifts in *Mary had a little lamb*. Incorporate scale-type shifts into familiar tunes with a small range; experiment with different ways of playing *Twinkle* or *Lavender's Blue* on one string only.

Play more target practice games: a short tune played with one finger shifting from note to note—good practice for awareness of tones and semitones (whole and half steps). Perhaps start with *Hot cross buns*. Play an arpeggio, starting on an open string, shifting on the 2nd or 4th finger and playing the octave harmonic for the top note. Sing and play a major scale by shifting on one finger, e.g.: 3 3 33 3 3 33.

Try these activities before and during learning to read music containing higher positions or shifts. The student becomes aware of the range of the violin and accustomed to playing stopped notes closer together as the string becomes shorter. Draw attention to the ease of playing groups of notes in a row with fingers in a row and the different tone colour of notes higher up a string. Developing this knowledge will lead towards natural position changes where they are musically and technically useful.

Position work and shifting basics

Teach new shifting techniques by rote, before using the written exercises. Check the student's thumb is flexible, its position isn't too high and that it stays in the same place relative to the fingers and is not left behind. Rather than stretching just one finger to a new position, shift the whole hand so the fingers meet the strings at approximately the same angle as in first position. Avoid gripping the neck so the hand may slide smoothly. Watch the wrist doesn't poke out while shifting. Shifting up, pull the upper arm in and let the elbow swing in, especially when shifting up the lower strings. Only the shifting finger should make contact with the string.

Sing or play tunes initially in 1st position to memorise the sound of the intervals, then play with shifts. Anticipate shifts by singing or mentally hearing the next note or notes. Feel the distance the left arm will move and lean towards the shift for a smooth start. Take time from the note before the shift so the target note is played on the beat.

Avoid jerkiness and faulty intonation by releasing thumb and finger pressure at the start of a shift and skating or skimming the shifting finger along the top of the string, (i.e. at harmonic pressure). Slow it down and listen as the target note is approached, thus stopping on the correct pitch to achieve accuracy every time and teaching the brain and muscles the exact distance. Lighten bow pressure and slightly slow the bow during shifts. If the pitch is inaccurate, don't wriggle your finger around looking for the missed note but stop and analyse. Too far? Not far enough? Then go back and take aim again.

When shifting to a different finger, no pitch higher than the two written notes should be audible. Emphasise the importance of the intermediate note (guide, bridge, auxiliary, grace or 'on-the-way' note) which is the guide to establishing the new position and good intonation. Play it deliberately at first to establish a good shifting technique, but it must ultimately be inaudible. The student can eventually learn to use the Romantic effect of *portamento*—and when, where and how much is musically appropriate.

Jennifer Thorp

Third position

Finger **1** takes finger **3**'s place.
Finger **2** takes finger **4**'s place.

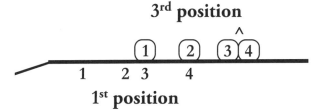

When shifting between 1st and 3rd position,
keep your fingers over the strings and slide your hand along the violin neck,
moving your whole arm to the new position.

D string

Practise shifting between 1st and 3rd position, with fingers **3** and **1** swapping places.
The sign ╱ tells you to shift up, ╲ to shift down.

Always check your
1st notes are in tune.

Pease pudding hot

Boil 'em cabbage down

American

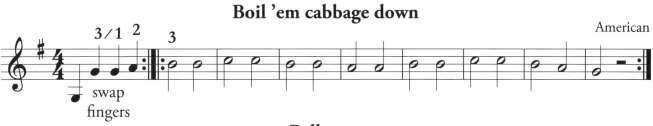

swap
fingers

Bell song

French

March

Test notes against open strings to make sure they are in tune.
Listen for the extra ring, open strings and notes that match them have, when you play in tune.

G major

Frère Jacques

French round

second voice starts

restez

This old man

Rigodon de Pelafol

French

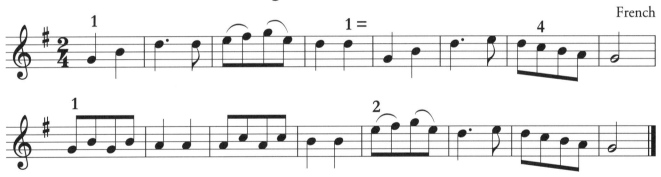

The dove

Russian

Turn again Whittington

second voice starts

English round

Drops of brandy
Irish jig

G major study

Some one
Check your first notes are in tune.

German

con sordino

Playing in G minor

Shalom chaverim
Israeli round

Remember stopped notes are closer together as the string becomes shorter.

D major

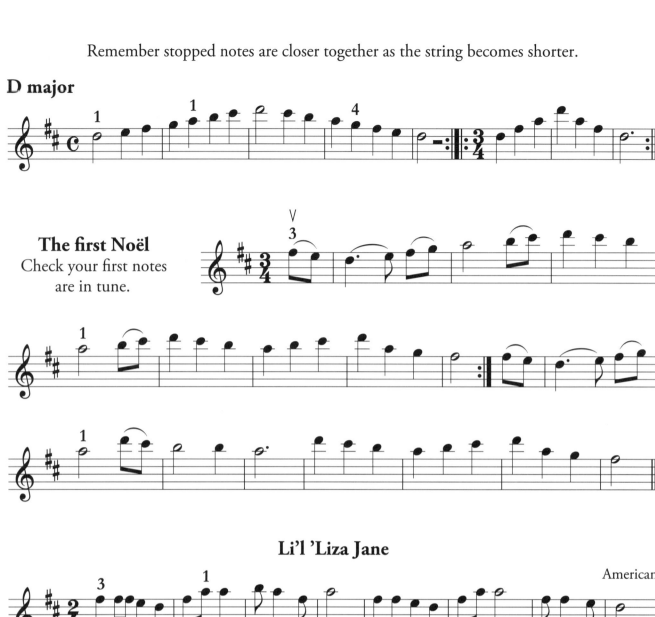

The first Noël
Check your first notes are in tune.

Li'l 'Liza Jane

American

Match D with the open string.

Sumer is icumen in
13C round

Each voice starts 2 bars after the previous voice.

Always check your
1st note is in tune.

D major study

Carillon
Round:
2nd voice starts
2 bars after 1st
voice.

Ah, poor bird
D minor:
play F natural.

D melodic minor

Staines morris dance

English

Galway Belle

Irish

D.S. al Fine

D harmonic minor

Marines' hymn
Always check your 1st note is in tune. Keep fingers down wherever possible.

American

C major 3rd finger changes its place in the second octave of C major.

Move your left elbow to match the string played, to help your fingers reach notes easily and accurately.

Dutch round

Broken thirds

Tum balalaika

Yiddish

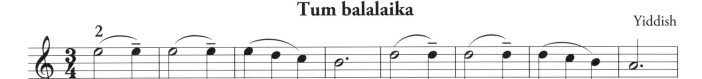

D major 4th finger changes its place in the second octave of D major.

White sand and grey sand

Round: 2nd voice starts 1 bar after 1st voice.

English

* backward extension
Keep hand in 3rd position and reach back with 1st finger.

Early to bed

American

Round: 2nd (3rd) voice starts 4 (8) bars after 1st voice.

Open string shifts

Change between 1st and 3rd positions while playing an open string.
When shifting, release thumb pressure and slide your hand along
the violin neck, moving your whole arm to the new position.

Afton water

Spilman

1. Play in 1st position.
2. Play with shifts.

restez

1. Play in 1st position.
2. Play with open string shifts.

When love is kind

Austrian

restez

Down in the valley

Shift during rests or while playing an open string.

Kentucky

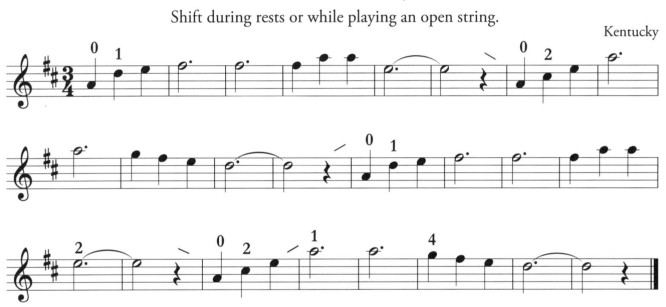

1. Play the arpeggios in 1st position.
2. Play with open string shifts.

G major   G minor

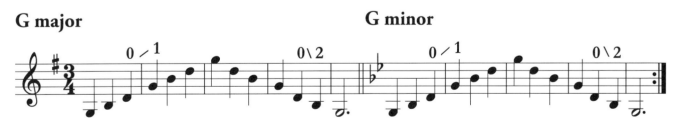

D major   D minor

Shifting between 1ˢᵗ and 3ʳᵈ positions on 1ˢᵗ finger

Shift with your **whole arm** to the new position.
1. **Release** thumb and finger pressure to **harmonic level**.
2. **Slide** 1ˢᵗ finger lightly and smoothly along the string.
3. **Listen** as it approaches the target note.
4. When you hear the target note, press finger down.

Release bow pressure and slow bow down during shift.

Sing and play.

Shifting with a bow change
new note, new bow

A string

Listen as finger **1** skates along the top of the string so you can stop in exactly the right place.

Gliding over arpeggios

Shifting with a bow change
new note, **new** bow

Camptown races

S Foster

1. Play in 1st position only.
2. Have fun fitting in lots of shifts.

D and A strings

I've been to Harlem

E string

Scottish air

D major

The shifting distance is greater when shifting from a **low 1ˢᵗ finger**.
Listen as you approach the new note so you can stop right on target.

D minor

G string
Keep your left elbow well under your violin.

1. Play in 1st position.
2. Play with G string shifts.

Patrick
Irish

1. Play in 1st position.
2. Play with shifts.

G major

G minor Shift further when starting from a low 1st finger.

Listen! On target? Too far? Not far enough?
Go back and take aim again, listening for your target note.
(Don't wriggle your finger around looking for the missed note.)

2nd finger shifts

Listen as 2nd finger approaches its new note so you can stop right on target.

E string

Blow the man down

Sea shanty

Skating around E string

Start shifting on the 'dot'.

Swing elbow well under violin.

G string

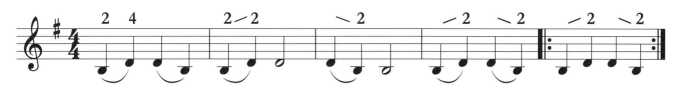

Li'l 'Liza Jane

American

Playing in F major.

new note,
new bow

Oh, Susannah

S Foster

Prepare: play the first three notes of F major on E string.

G string

Keep elbow well under violin.

Les marionnettes

French

A string
4th finger shifts

Goal shooting

Harmonics

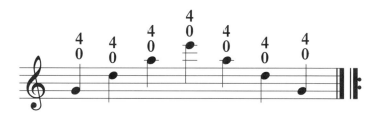

These notes are half-way along each string.
When playing harmonics from 3rd position:
1. **Keep** your thumb and hand in position.
2. **Extend** your 4th finger.
3. Lightly **touch** the string.
4. Bow closer to the bridge.
Swing your left elbow under your violin
to match the string being played.

Play an arpeggio each way on each string.

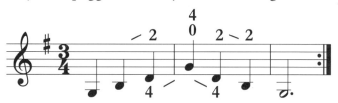

Mainly E string stretches

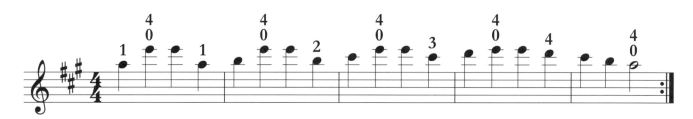

Savez-vous planter les choux

French

Oranges and lemons

Swing left elbow well under violin.

Bell horses

Changing position from 1st finger to another finger

Hear or imagine the note you are shifting to.
1. **Shift on the last** (**the old**) **finger**, shown as a finger number above a line,
to the 'on-the-way' (guide or bridge) note, shown as a grace-note.
2. Play the **target note** with the **new finger**.
At first, sound the guide note. With practice, this note will become silent.

A minor moves

1. Play in 1st position.
2. Play with shifts.

Change finger, change bow

1. **Shift** on the **old finger** on the **old bow**.
2. Play the **new finger** and **note** with the **new bow**.

Kemo, kimo

A string

Playing in B♭ major.

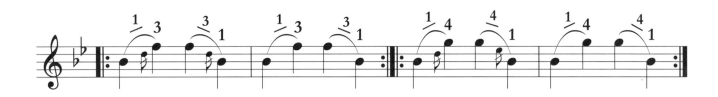

1. Play tunes in 1st position.
2. Play with shifts.

Waltzing around A string

Change finger, change bow

1. Shift on the **old finger** on the **old bow**.
2. Play the **new finge**r and **note** with the **new bow**.

Haste to the wedding

Irish jig

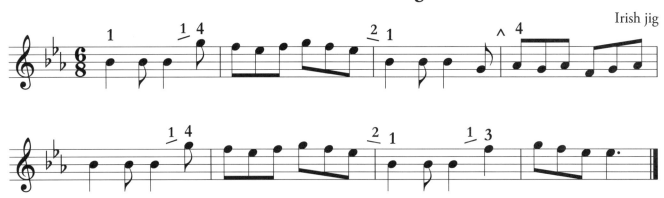

Listen! On target? Too far? Not far enough?
Go back and take aim again, listening for your target note.
(Don't wiggle your finger around to find a missed note.)

E string

When shifting to a different finger:
1. **Shift** on the **old finger** to the guide or 'on-the-way' note.
2. Play the **new note** with the **new finger**.

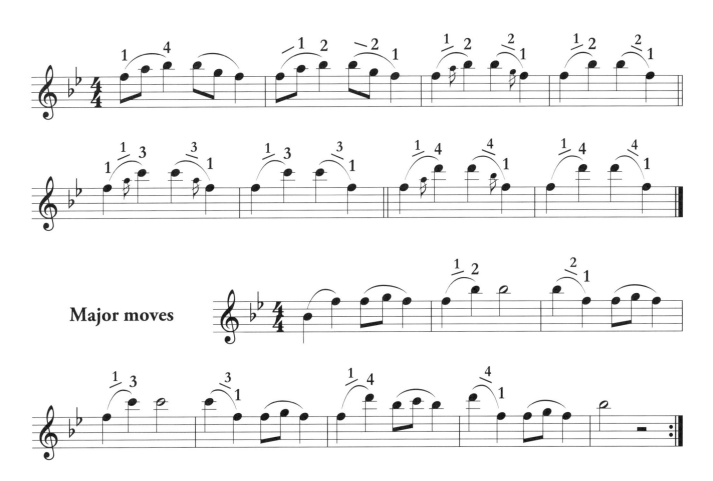

Major moves

Change finger, change bow

1. Shift on the **old finger** on the **old bow**.
2. Play the **new note** with the **new bow**.

Arkansas traveller

American

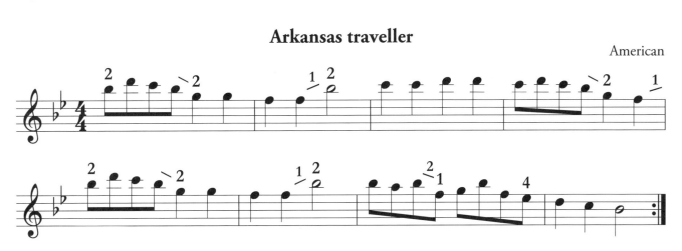

G string

Swing elbow well under violin.

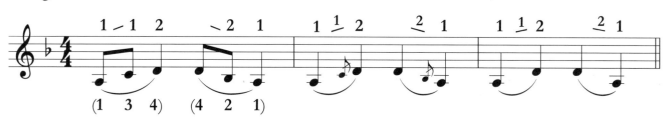

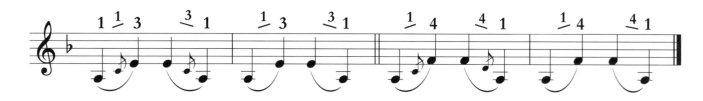

D minor moves

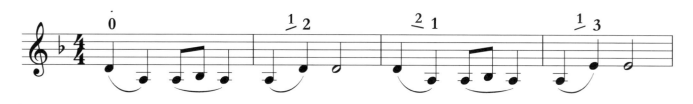

Change finger, change bow

Shifty moves

More position changes to a different finger

Hear or imagine the note you are shifting to.

When shifting to a different finger:
1. **Shift** on the **old finger**, shown as a finger number above a line,
   to the guide or 'on-the-way' note, shown as a grace-note.
2. Play the **target note** with the **new finger**.
   At first sound the guide note. With practice this note will become silent.

D string

New finger, new bow

The seeker

Round

A string

new finger, **new** bow

E string

change finger, **change** bow

My journey home

American

Listen! On target? Too far? Not far enough?
Go back and take aim again, listening for your target note.
(Don't wiggle your finger around to find a missed note.)

Shifting up or down a step (a scale shift)

The grace-note won't be audible but is a guide to the shifting finger.

Shift up on the **new finger**.
Finger **1** pushes finger **2** out of the way.

Stepping up, sliding down

Shift up
new finger,
new bow

Shift down
on the **old finger**.

Swap 1 for 2.

Stepping down

C major
new finger,
new bow

Ce fut en mai

Trad. French, adap.

C major shifts study

Shift up on the **new finger**.
Finger **2** pushes finger **3** out of the way.

Robin Adair

Scottish

Shift down on the **old finger**.

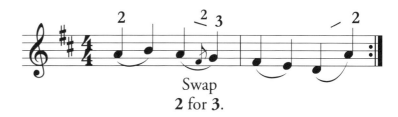

Swap **2** for **3**.

D major

New finger, **new** bow

Shift **up** on **new** finger.   Shift **down** on **old** finger.

31

A string scale shifts

Shift **up** on **new** finger.   Shift **down** on **old** finger.

Scottiche gasconne

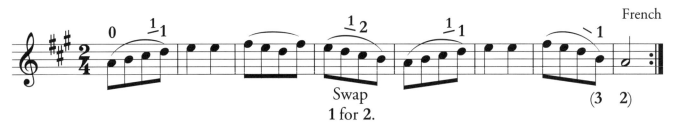

French

Swap **1** for **2**.   (3 2)

A major **new** finger, **new** bow

Shift **up** on **new** finger.   Shift **down** on **old** finger.

New finger, **new** bow

Swap **2** for **3**.

Lover's whims

restez   *restez*

restez

E string scale shifts

Shift **up** on the **new** finger.
Shift **down** on the **old** finger.

Miska and Panni

Hungarian

Round

2nd voice starts when
1st voice reaches bar 3.

D major shifts study

Shift while changing bow.

D major Experiment with shifting in different places on different strings.

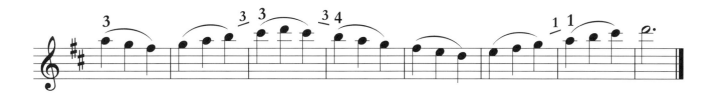

E major

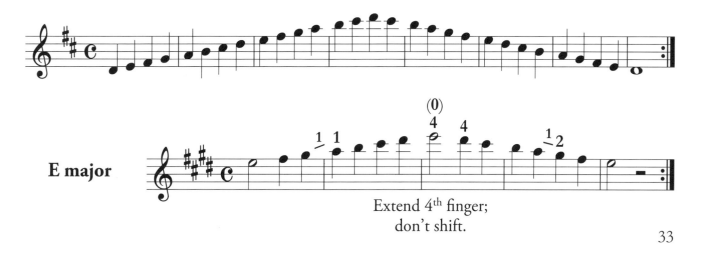

Extend 4th finger;
don't shift.

33

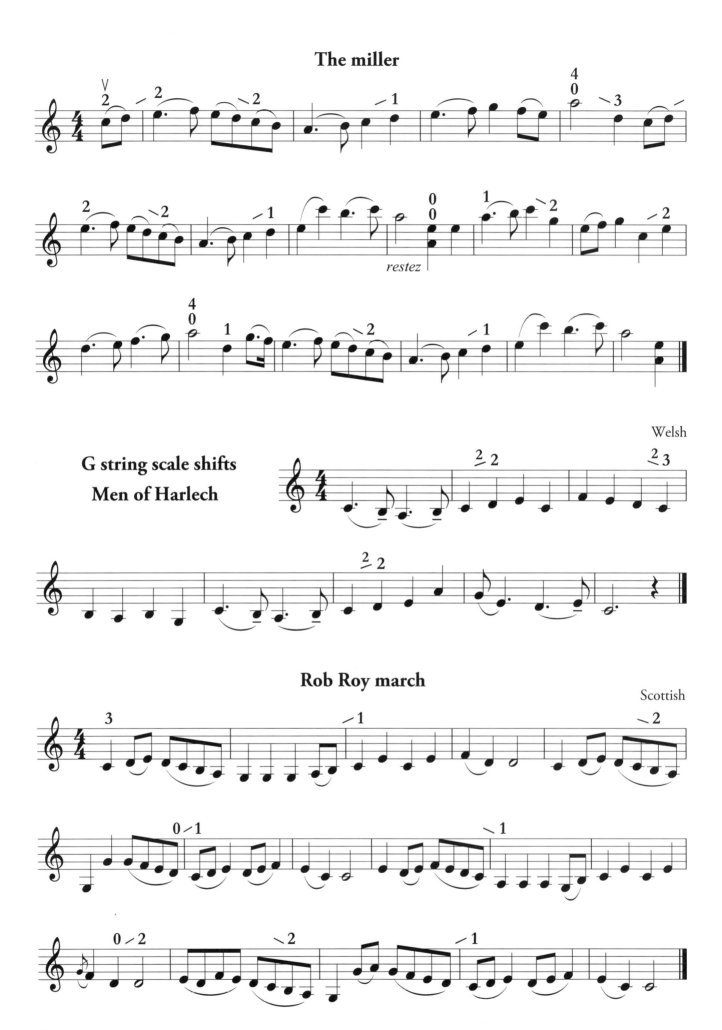

Shift between fingered notes across strings

Imagine or hear the notes you are shifting to.
1. **Shift** on the **old finger** and **string**.
2. **New finger** crosses over to **new string** and **new note**.
   No higher pitch than the two written notes should be heard.

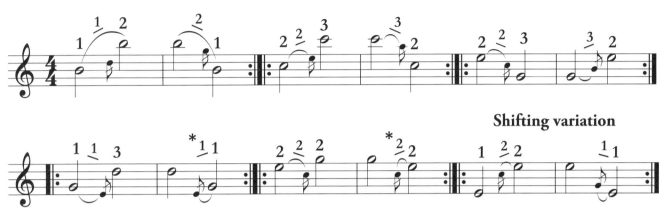

* These new notes need to be approached **from below**, so shift on the **new finger** on the **new string**.

Shifting variation

Shift on the **new finger** for a more expressive effect where musically appropriate.

* Try shifting up D string on 1ˢᵗ finger, then up A string on 2ⁿᵈ finger and listen for which shift you prefer.

Portsmouth

English

French air

Charles Chaulieu

Shift up D string.

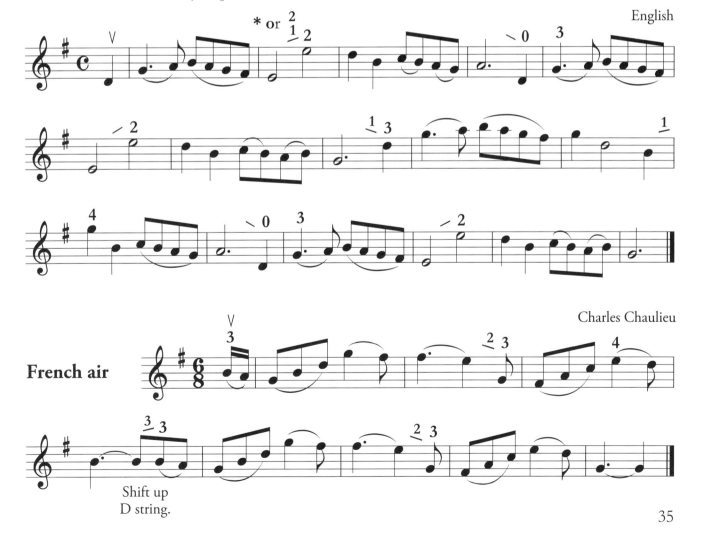

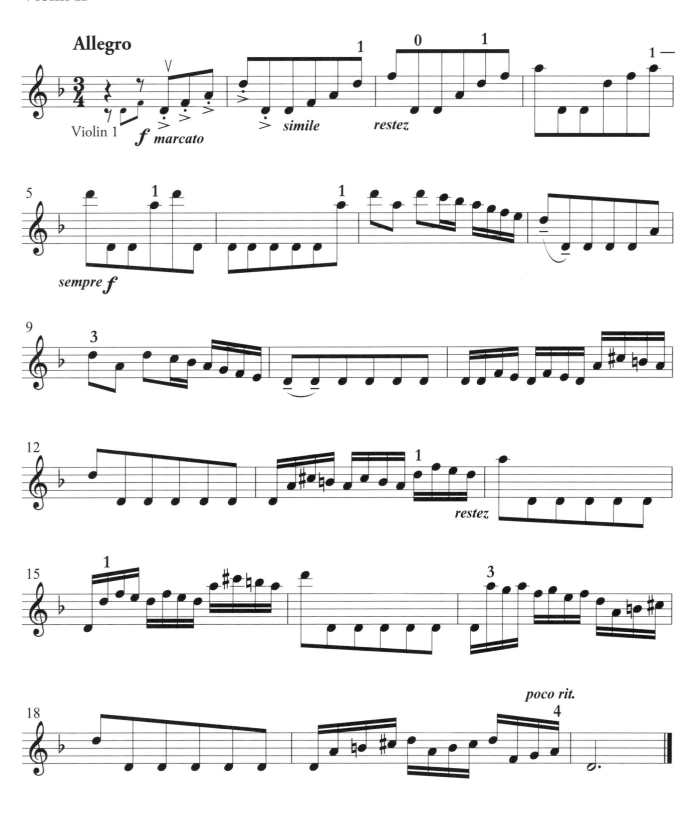

Second position

Finger **1** takes finger **2**'s place.
Check notes against open strings
to help you stay in tune.
Listen for the extra ring, open strings
and notes that match them
have, when you play in tune.

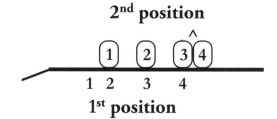

Move your whole arm up to 2nd position.

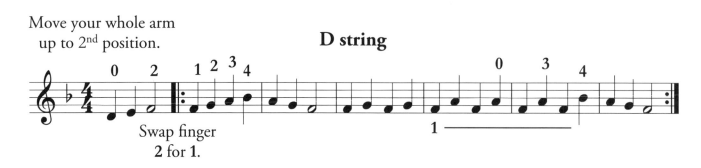

Swap finger 2 for 1.

Match A with the open string.

Boil 'em cabbage down
American

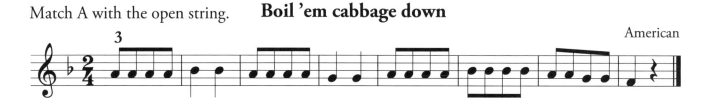

F major

Now the day is over
Baring-Gould

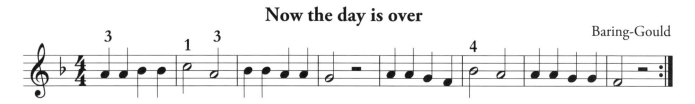

French folk song

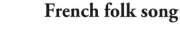

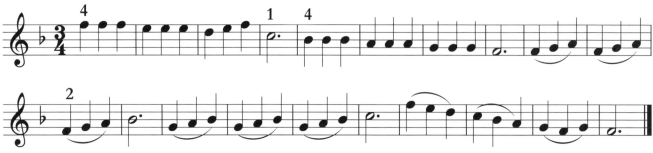

Carillon
2nd voice starts 2 bars after 1st voice.

Round

E string

If you want to try these tunes in 1st position, stretch up to high C without shifting your hand.

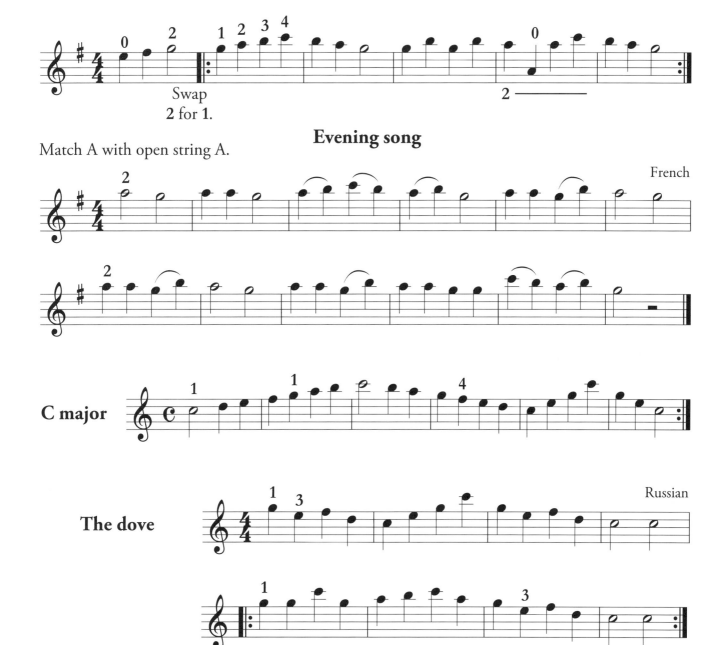

Evening song

Match A with open string A.

C major

The dove

Rigodon de Pelafol

G string

Move your whole arm up to 2nd position.

B flat major

Match D to the open string.

There is a happy land
American Indian

The billygoat
Russian

B flat major study

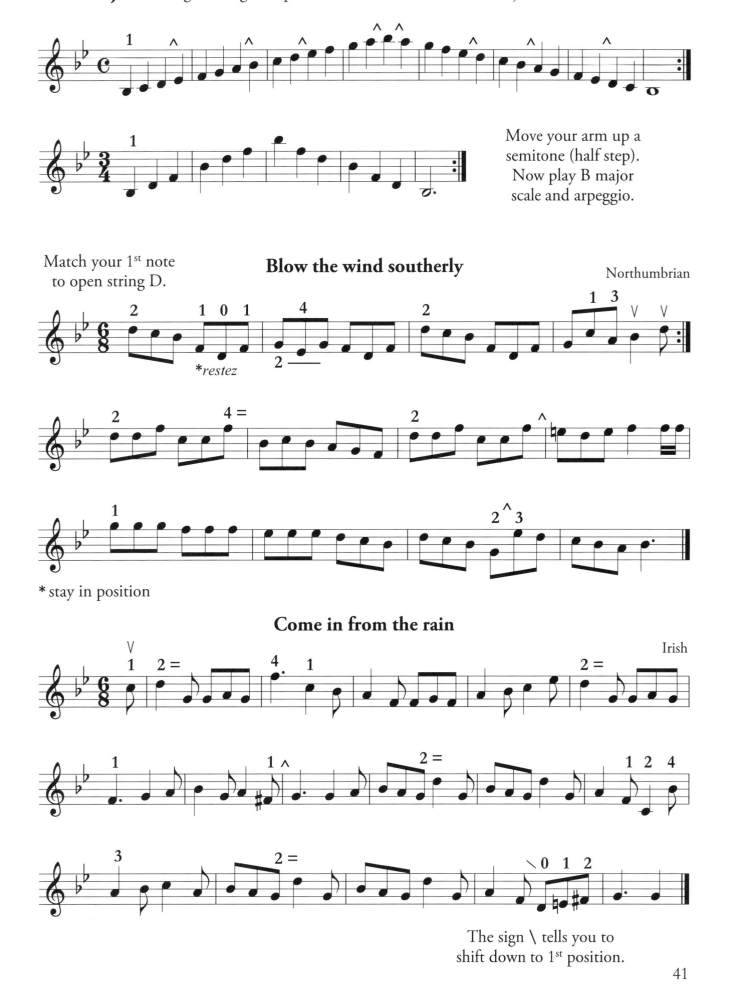

C major 4th finger changes its place in the 2nd octave of C major.

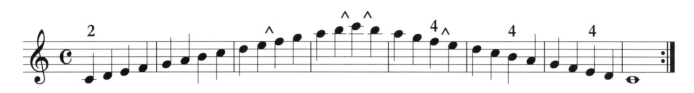

Move your left elbow to match the string played, to help your fingers reach notes easily and accurately.

Over the hills and far away

English

Highland laddie

Scottish

Music in 1st and 2nd positions

When shifting to another position:
your arm, hand and thumb move together.
Release thumb and finger pressure on the string, slide
lightly and smoothly along the top of the string.
Listen as you approach the target note and
when you hear it, press finger down.

Old King Cole

On a bank of flowers

Scottish

Music in 1st, 2nd and 3rd positions